DATE DUE

GAYLORD			PRINTED IN U.S.A.

PowerKids Readers:

The Bilingual Library of the United States of America™

KANSAS

JOSÉ MARÍA OBREGÓN

TRADUCCIÓN AL ESPAÑOL: MARÍA CRISTINA BRUSCA

The Rosen Publishing Group's
PowerKids Press™ & **Editorial Buenas Letras**™
New York

Published in 2006 by The Rosen Publishing Group, Inc.
29 East 21st Street, New York, NY 10010

First Edition

Photo Credits: Cover, p. 31 (Grassland) © Philip Gould/Corbis; p. 5 © Joe Sohm/The Image Works; p. 7 © 2002 Geoatlas; pp. 9, 17, 19, 31 (Love, Johnson, Eisenhower, Earhart, Brooks) © Bettmann/Corbis; p.11 © Jon Davies/Jim Reed Photography/Corbis; pp. 13, 15, 31 (Buffalo) Library of Congress Prints and Photographs Division; p. 21 Copyright 2005 Vic Bilson; p. 23 © Jim Sugar/Corbis; pp. 25, 30 (Capital) © Richard Cummins/Corbis; pp. 26, 30 (Wild Sunflower, Sunflower State) © Japack Company/Corbis; p. 30 (Western Meadowlark) © Darrell Gulin/Corbis; p. 30 (Cottonwood) © Richard A. Cooke/Corbis; p. 31 (Keaton) © John Springer Collection/Corbis; p. 31 (Drought) © William James Warren/Corbis.

Library of Congress Cataloging-in-Publication Data

Obregón, José María, 1963–
Kansas / José María Obregón ; traducción al español, María Cristina Brusca: María Cristina Brusca.— 1st ed.
p. cm. — (The bilingual library of the United States of America) Includes bibliographical references (p.) and index.
ISBN 1-4042-3081-5 (library binding)
1. Kansas–Juvenile literature. I. Title. II. Series.
F681.3.O27 2005
978.1—dc22

2005006101

Manufactured in the United States of America

Due to the changing nature of Internet links, Editorial Buenas Letras has developed an online list of Web sites related to the subject of this book. This site is updated regularly. Please use this link to access the list:

http://www.buenasletraslinks.com/ls/kansas

Contents

Contenido

Welcome to Kansas

These are the flag and the seal of Kansas. Kansas is known as the Sunflower State. The sunflower is Kansas's state flower. You can see a sunflower in the flag.

Bienvenidos a Kansas

Estos son la bandera y el escudo de Kansas. Kansas es conocido como el Estado del Girasol. El girasol es la flor del estado de Kansas. En la bandera puedes ver un girasol.

Kansas Flag and State Seal

Bandera y escudo de Kansas

Kansas Geography

Kansas borders the states of Colorado, Nebraska, Missouri, and Oklahoma. Kansas is rectangular in shape. Only its northeast border has an uneven shape.

Geografía de Kansas

Kansas está limitado por los estados de Colorado, Nebraska, Misuri y Oklahoma. Kansas tiene forma de rectángulo. Solamente en el noreste la frontera tiene una forma irregular.

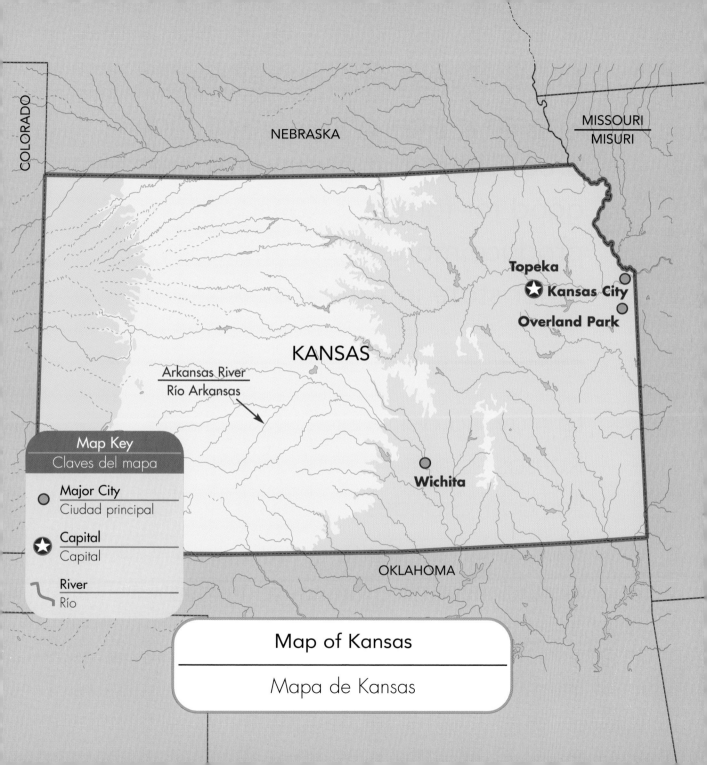

COLORADO

NEBRASKA

MISSOURI
MISURI

Topeka
★ Kansas City
Overland Park

KANSAS

Arkansas River
Río Arkansas

Wichita

Map Key
Claves del mapa

Major City
Ciudad principal

Capital
Capital

River
Río

OKLAHOMA

Map of Kansas

Mapa de Kansas

Much of western and central Kansas is part of the Great Plains area. These flat grasslands are good for farming. Kansas's farms produce more wheat than any other state in America.

La mayoría del centro y el oeste de Kansas es parte de una región llamada Grandes Llanuras. Esta llanura es muy buena para la agricultura y la ganadería. Las granjas de Kansas producen más trigo que cualquier otro estado de los Estados Unidos.

Farming Wheat in Lyons, Kansas
_____
Cosecha de trigo en Lyons, Kansas

Kansas has hard weather. Winters can be very cold, and summers can be very hot. Natural events like tornadoes, droughts, and floods are common throughout the state.

Kansas tiene un clima muy duro. Los inviernos pueden ser muy fríos y los veranos pueden ser muy calurosos. Los fenómenos naturales, como los tornados, inundaciones y sequías, son comunes en todas partes del estado.

Tornado Touching Down in Clearwater, Kansas

Un tornado toca tierra en Clearwater, Kansas

Kansas History

The name "Kansas" comes from the Kansa or Kaw nation. The Kansa, the Comanche, the Sioux, and other Native American nations have lived in Kansas since the 1750s. They were buffalo hunters.

Historia de Kansas

El nombre "Kansas" viene del nombre de la nación Kansa o Kaw. Las naciones Kansa, Comanche, Sioux y otras naciones de nativos americanos han vivido en Kansas desde 1750. Estos nativos eran cazadores de búfalos.

Buffalo Hunters, 1890–1900

Cazadores de búfalos, 1890–1900

In the 1850s, Kansans wanted to allow slavery in the state. Others thought slavery should be banned. John Brown fought most of his life to end slavery. Thanks to his work slavery was banned in Kansas in 1859.

En la década de 1850, algunos kanseños quisieron permitir la esclavitud en el estado. Otros pensaban que la esclavitud debería de estar prohibida. John Brown luchó casi toda su vida para terminar con la esclavitud. Gracias a su trabajo, la esclavitud fue prohibida en Kansas en 1859.

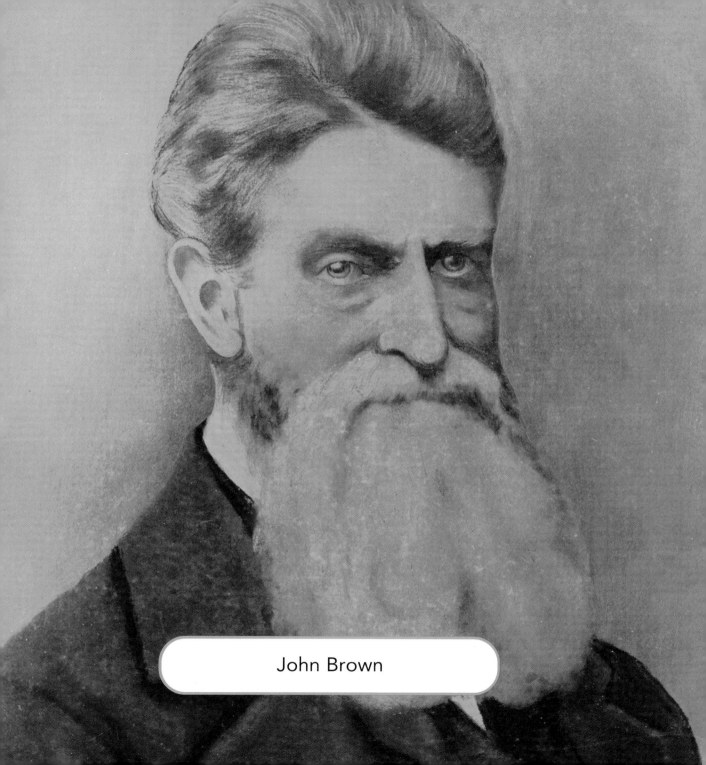

John Brown

Cattle drives from Texas to Kansas were common in the 1870s. Cowboys worked moving animals from one state to the other. Cattle drives brought many cowboys to Kansas.

Los arreos de ganado, desde Texas a Kansas, fueron comunes durante la década de 1870. Los vaqueros trabajaban llevando los animales de uno a otro estado. Los arreos de ganado atrajeron a muchos vaqueros a Kansas.

Cattle Drive in Kansas, 1949

Arreo de ganado en Kansas, 1949

Amelia Earhart was born in Atchison, Kansas, in 1897. In 1928, she became the first woman to fly across the Atlantic Ocean as a passenger. Five years later she became the first woman to fly alone across the Atlantic in an airplane.

Amelia Earhart nació en Atchison, Kansas, en 1897. En 1928, fue la primera mujer en volar a través del océano Atlántico, como pasajera de un avión. Cinco años más tarde, Earhart fue la primer mujer en cruzar el Atlántico volando sola en un aeroplano.

Amelia Earhart

Living in Kansas

Kansans know how to have fun. During the River Festival in Wichita participants race across the Arkansas River. They race in antique bathtubs or in odd-looking rafts.

La vida en Kansas

Los kanseños saben cómo divertirse. Durante el Festival del Río, en Wichita, los participantes compiten en una carrera, cruzando el río Arkansas. Los participantes compiten navegando en bañeras antiguas o en balsas de aspecto curioso.

The Bathtub Race

Carrera de bañeras

Many Kansans work in the airplane industry. These Kansans make airplanes. Important airplane companies like Cessna and Boeing are located in Kansas.

Muchos kanseños trabajan en la industria de la aviación. Estos kanseños construyen aviones. Importantes fábricas de aviones, como Cessna y Boeing están establecidas en Kansas.

Airplane Factory in Wichita, Kansas

Fábrica de aviones en Wichita, Kansas

Wichita, Overland Park, Kansas City, and Topeka are important cities in Kansas. Topeka is the capital of Kansas.

Wichita, Overland Park, Kansas City y Topeka son ciudades importantes de Kansas. Topeka es la capital de Kansas.

Kansas State Capitol Building

Capitolio del estado de Kansas

Activity:
Let's Draw the Kansas State Flower
The Wild Sunflower became the Kansas state flower in 1903.

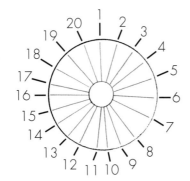

Actividad: Dibujemos la flor del estado de Kansas
El girasol silvestre es la flor del estado de Kansas desde 1903.

1

Draw a small circle for the center of the flower. Draw a larger circle around the first one.

Dibuja un círculo pequeño en el lugar del centro de la flor. Dibuja un círculo más grande alrededor del primero.

2

Draw 20 lines from the small circle to the second circle.

Dibuja 20 líneas desde el círculo pequeño hasta el segundo círculo.

3

Erase the large circle.

Borra el círculo más grande.

4

Draw the tips of the petals using an upside-down *V*.

Dibuja las puntas de los pétalos en forma de *V* invertida.

5

Keep adding the *V*'s. Draw lines from the ends of each *V* to the center.

Sigue agregando esas formas de *V*. Traza líneas desde el final de cada V hasta el centro.

6

Finish the petals. Add a stem. Add shading and detail to the flower.

Termina los pétalos. Añade un tallo. Agrega sombras y detalles a tu flor.

Timeline

Cronología

René-Robert Cavelier de La Salle claims the area west of the Mississippi River for France. That includes Kansas.	**1682**	René-Robert Cavelier de La Salle reclama para Francia la tierra al oeste del río Misisipi. Kansas está incluída en estos territorios.
Kansas is purchased by the United States as part of the Louisiana Purchase.	**1803**	La región de Kansas es comprada por los Estados Unidos como parte de la Compra de Luisiana.
The Santa Fe trail is established.	**1822**	Se establece la Ruta de Santa Fe.
Conflicts begin between proslavery and antislavery forces.	**1855**	Comienzan los conflictos entre partidarios y opositores a la esclavitud.
Kansas becomes the thirty-fourth state of the Union.	**1861**	Kansas se convierte en el estado treinta y cuatro de la Unión.
The U.S. Supreme Court rules that racially segregated schools are illegal.	**1954**	La Suprema Corte de los Estados Unidos declara ilegal la segregación racial en las escuelas.

Kansas Events

January
International Pancake Day
in Liberal

March
Kansas Special Olympics
in Wichita

April
Eisenhower Center Open House
in Abilene

May
Wichita River Festival

June
Flint Hills Rodeo in Strong City

July
Mexican Fiesta in Topeka
Dodge City Days

September
Kansas State Fair in Hutchinson
North Central Kansas Fair
in Belleville

December
Christmas at the Museum in Wichita

Eventos en Kansas

Enero
Festival internacional del panqueque, en
Liberal

Marzo
Olimpíadas Especiales de Kansas, en
Wichita

Abril
Día de puertas abiertas en el Centro
Eisenhower, en Abilene

Mayo
Festival del Río en Wichita

Junio
Rodeo de Flint Hills, en Strong City

Julio
Fiesta mexicana, en Topeka
Días de Dodge City

Septiembre
Feria del estado de Kansas, en Hutchinson
Feria del norte y centro de Kansas, en
Belleville

Diciembre
Navidad en el museo, en Wichita

Kansas Facts/Datos sobre Kansas

<u>Population</u> 2.6 million		<u>Población</u> 2.6 millones
<u>Capital</u> Topeka		<u>Capital</u> Topeka
<u>State Motto</u> To the Stars Through Difficulties		<u>Lema del estado</u> Hacia las estrellas a través de las dificultades
<u>State Flower</u> Wild sunflower		<u>Flor del estado</u> Girasol silvestre
<u>State Bird</u> Western meadowlark		<u>Ave del estado</u> perdigón
<u>State Nickname</u> The Sunflower State		<u>Mote del estado</u> El Estado del Girasol
<u>State Tree</u> Cottonwood		<u>Árbol del estado</u> Álamo
<u>State Song</u> "Home on the Range"		<u>Canción del estado</u> "Hogar en la pradera"

Famous Kansans/Kanseños famosos

Nat Love
(1854–1925)

Cowboy
Vaquero

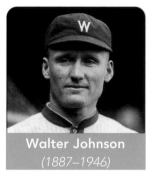

Walter Johnson
(1887–1946)

Baseball player
Jugador de béisbol

Dwight D. "Ike" Eisenhower
(1890–1969)

U.S. President
Presidente de E.U.A.

Buster Keaton
(1895–1966)

Silent film star
Estrella del cine mudo

Amelia Earhart
(1895–1966)

Aviator
Aviadora

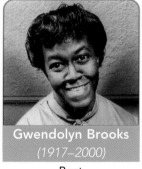

Gwendolyn Brooks
(1917–2000)

Poet
Poeta

Words to Know/Palabras que debes saber

border
frontera

buffalo
búfalo

drought
sequía

grassland
pradera

Here are more books to read about Kansas:
Otros libros que puedes leer sobre Kansas:

In English/En inglés:

Kansas, It's My State!
By King, G. David
Benchmark Books, 2004

Kansas
Hello USA
by Fredeen, Charles
Lerner Publications, 2002

Words in English: 315

Palabras en español: 375

Index

Índice